PUCKSTER'S FIRST HOCKEY TRYOUT

CANADA

FENN

TUNDRA

PUCKSTER

BY LORNA SCHULTZ NICHOLSON
ILLUSTRATED BY KELLY FINDLEY

Puckster jiggled his legs as he sat in the hockey arena's dressing room. His stomach flip-flopped. Sweat ran down his forehead.

Today he was trying out for a special hockey team. This team would play one big game against the Russian Tigers, and it was going to be on television. Puckster knew that only half the players trying out would make the team.

Puckster glanced at his teammates. They were all trying out, too. Roly bit his nails. Charlie bounced around the bench like a Ping-Pong ball. Sarah listened to music. Manny scratched his antlers. Francois flapped his tail on the floor. And Yuan shook as he hid under the bench.

Puckster wanted all his friends to make the team so they could play together.

"The ice is ready!" yelled the coach. Puckster checked to make sure his laces were done up tightly.

Puckster stood up and gave his friends high fives. Everyone looked really nervous. They quietly made their way out to the rink.

Even though his knees were shaking, Puckster stepped on the ice with confidence. He skated around and around the rink. He placed his stick behind his back to warm up. He did crossovers as he skated around the corners, and he took some shots on net. Sarah and Manny skated along with him and did everything that he did.

Roly didn't warm up with Puckster, Sarah, and Manny. Instead, he drank water at the bench.

"Do you want to skate with us?" Puckster asked Roly. "It helps warm up our muscles."

Roly shook his head. "Nope," he said. "I don't like warming up."

The coach blew his whistle. "Get into two lines at the far end of the ice," he called out.

Puckster skated fast. He wanted to be first in line to show he was keen. Charlie skated as fast as he could and was first in line, too.

Puckster listened to the coach as he explained the drill.

Charlie didn't listen. He kept spinning around. He talked to the player behind him. Puckster wanted to tell Charlie to listen, but he couldn't because he had to listen to the coach.

The whistle blew and Puckster knew exactly what to do. Charlie didn't.

The drill had just started when the whistle shrieked again. Everyone stopped. The coach pointed to Charlie. "Go to the back of the line and watch so you will know what to do," he said.

Charlie hung his head. He wished he had listened to the coach.

The next time the whistle blew, the players took turns skating down the ice. They stopped and started at each line.

When all the forwards and defence had completed the drill, it was time for Manny to have his turn with the other sled players.

Puckster watched Manny dig his hockey sticks into the ice and push and push. "Go, Manny!" Puckster cheered.

When he was finished, Manny panted and could hardly catch his breath. He had finished last.

Puckster patted his shoulder. "Good work," he said. "You tried hard."

The goalies were the last group of players to do the drill. Roly took off like a big gust of wind. He was a speedy skater.

"Go, Roly!" Puckster cheered.

Roly screeched to a stop at the blue line. Then he pushed his legs to skate forward again. When he got to the red line, he stopped so quickly, his blades sprayed ice.

Suddenly, Roly fell and rolled around on the ice. He grabbed the back of his leg. "Ouch! Ouch!" he cried. Roly had pulled a muscle.

The trainer ran across the ice in his running shoes.

Puckster felt sad for Roly as the trainer helped him hobble off the ice. Roly should have warmed up.

When all the skating drills were over, it was time to play a game. Puckster skated to the bench for some water. His heart raced. His legs trembled. He wiped the sweat from his brow, took a deep breath, and drank some water. Then he snapped the top back in place.

Manny drank his water too, but his hands shook and he spilled some on his jersey. Sarah skated nervously back and forth as she drank her water. And Francois didn't drink any water because he sat on the ice with his head between his legs.

The coach blew his whistle to start the game. Francois quickly skated to his wing position. Puckster skated to centre ice for the face-off. The puck dropped and the game started.

Puckster tried to remember everything the coach said. When his shift was over, he skated to the bench. Yuan had his skates off.

"It's your turn to play," Puckster said to Yuan.

Yuan shook his head. "I don't want to try out anymore. I don't care if I'm on television. I just want to play on our house-league team."

"But you did all the drills," said Puckster.

"I know, but I don't want to play with that team."

Puckster smiled at his friend. "That's okay," he said. "No matter which team you play for, you're still playing hockey."

Yuan smiled at Puckster. "I want you to make it, Puckster. I know how important it is to you."

By the end of the game, Puckster and Sarah had both scored two goals. Manny had worked hard on defence but didn't score. Francois was so tired and thirsty that he could hardly skate. He should have drunk some water.

When the tryout was over, the coach talked to each player individually.

"Congratulations, Puckster," said the coach. "You made the team."

Puckster raced out to tell his friends, but when he saw them, he was scared to share his good news.

What if they hadn't made it?

"Did you make the team?" his friends asked.

Puckster slowly nodded.

"You deserve it, Puckster," said Francois.

"You worked hard for this," said Roly.

"Yeah!" cheered the rest of his friends.

A big grin spread across Puckster's face.

"Sarah made it, too!" squeaked Charlie.

Puckster high-fived Sarah. Then he looked at Manny. Puckster knew Manny had done everything right but still hadn't made the team.

Manny sat up tall. "The coach told me to keep trying. Maybe I can make it next year."

"You sure can," encouraged Puckster.

When the time came for the big game, Puckster and Sarah saw all their friends in the stands. They held a magnificent banner that read, "Go, Puckster! Go, Sarah!"
And with their big banner, all of Puckster's friends were shown on television!

PUCKSTER'S TIPS:

Make sure to listen to your coach!

Warm up your muscles before practicing or playing in a game.

Always bring your own water bottle to your hockey practices and games. You can't play your best if you are thirsty!

If you don't make the team you are trying out for, don't give up!

PUCKSTER'S HOCKEY TIP:

When taking a **face-off**, bend your knees and hold the stick with one hand on the top and the other really low on the shaft. As the referee drops the puck, **keep your eye on the puck** and react with your stick as quickly as possible.

Good luck!